INSPIRED BY TRUE EVENTS

Evan Phạm

the woman of the weeping wilderness

聖 母 越 南

Truyền Thuyết Đức Mẹ La Vang
The Legend of Our Lady of La Vang

Holy Smack Press [formerly Banned Books Press]
Detroit, Michigan, USA

NOTICE:

This novelette depicts scenes of violent persecution and
is intended for mature readers, preferably young adults and older.

-READER DISCRETION IS ADVISED-

For Mary – the World's First Love

totus tuus

ACKNOWLEDGEMENTS

Firstly, I am grateful to the Holy Trinity for gifting me everything I have and am to glorify Him with this work, which includes my parents, my sister and her family, my brother and his, my godchildren and their families, my many friends and teachers, and my many former students (and their families) who have become beloved friends.

Particularly, I thank the late Deacon Xavier Đoàn Ngọc Châu, whose master's thesis on Đức Mẹ La Vang (at Sacred Heart Major Seminary, Detroit) inspired me to tell Our Blessed Mother's story as beautifully as I could.

I thank my father and the Việt community he raised me in, which fed me in ways I am still discovering. I thank all my friends in Phong Trào Thiếu Nhi Thánh Thể, specifically Đoàn Anrê Trần Anh Dũng, my home chapter. I am indebted to these priests for their ministry and care: Reverends Lâm, Nguyễn, Peterman, Ward, and White.

I also thank those who will read this work, and all who provided feedback and support during revising, especially: Dr. Philip Blosser, Lonnie and Glenis Collins, Hưng và Diễm Đinh, Khoa Nguyễn, Coleen Redmond, Kristen Wolocko, and Andrew Zoratti.

Lastly, I thank my dear friend Lan, whose presence in my life inspired the character of the same name, and whose discernment and sacrifice made this work possible.

May our Lady keep us all near her Son.

Preface

Imperial Việt Nam's persecution of the Catholic Church starting in the late 1700s, and the miraculous Marian apparition they witnessed, deserved better than the briefly recorded and vague accounts in English that I heard growing up as a Việtnamese-American. With this novelette, I sought to bring together and elaborate the details, cultural practices, and historical setting, all presented in one dramatic tale. In short, I searched for a legend of Our Lady of La Vang that I would want to read for myself and eagerly share with others, but since there was none, I took the matter into my own hands and imagination. May I now present my best effort: *The Woman of the Weeping Wilderness*; I hope I have honored our Blessed Mother, her Son, and her Việtnamese children.

Regarding Việtnamese language: the Latin script used today in Việtnamese, and featured in this novelette, was first introduced in Việt Nam by Catholic missionaries in the 1600s. Prior to this, and due to a millennium of Chinese colonization, Việtnamese was merely written in Chinese characters, but within a distinct Việtnamese syntax and pronunciation system. At the risk of being anachronistic, the Latinized Việtnamese script is presented here in this novelette to recognize the lasting efforts of Catholic missionaries on the culture, and the contemporary Việtnamese people who have inherited this unique gift. Việtnamese remains the sole East Asian language to have adopted the Latin alphabet as its official script.

Additionally, being a tonal based language, the tone of a vowel (noted with written accent marks, such as: é, è, ẻ, ẽ, ẹ) changes the meaning of a word entirely. Thus, despite my best attempts to provide pronunciation guides in the footnotes, most of my suggestions remain merely approximate and rough. To further complicate matters, Việtnamese has 12 written vowels: ă, â, a, ê, e, i, ô, ơ, o, ư, u, and y – some with no English equivalent.

Regarding the historical setting: the story centers on a family of an unnamed village in the vicinity of current-day La Vang, near the ancient capital city of Huế, Việt Nam, in the nation's Central Region (Miền Trung). At that time, La Vang was a remote area of uninhabited, mountainous wilderness where Christians desperately hid to escape violence from anti-Christian forces. Believed to have been haunted, the place gained its name "La Vang" because of a pun inherent in how the phrase is tonally pronounced, changing its meaning: *La Vang* (to cry out and weep) or *Lá Vằng* (the leaf of a specific local medicinal plant). Both meanings apply to the Marian apparition of 1798, as the story will unfold.

Almost 200 years later, in 1988, Pope St. John Paul II canonized 117 Martyrs of Việt Nam. Their Feast Day is November 24th on the Novus Ordo liturgical calendar.

Speaking of liturgy, the Roman Catholic prayers and rituals presented here are historically accurate with that time period's practice of worshiping God through the ancient Traditional Latin Mass, and with the Church's official tongue (see LatinMass.com for much more).

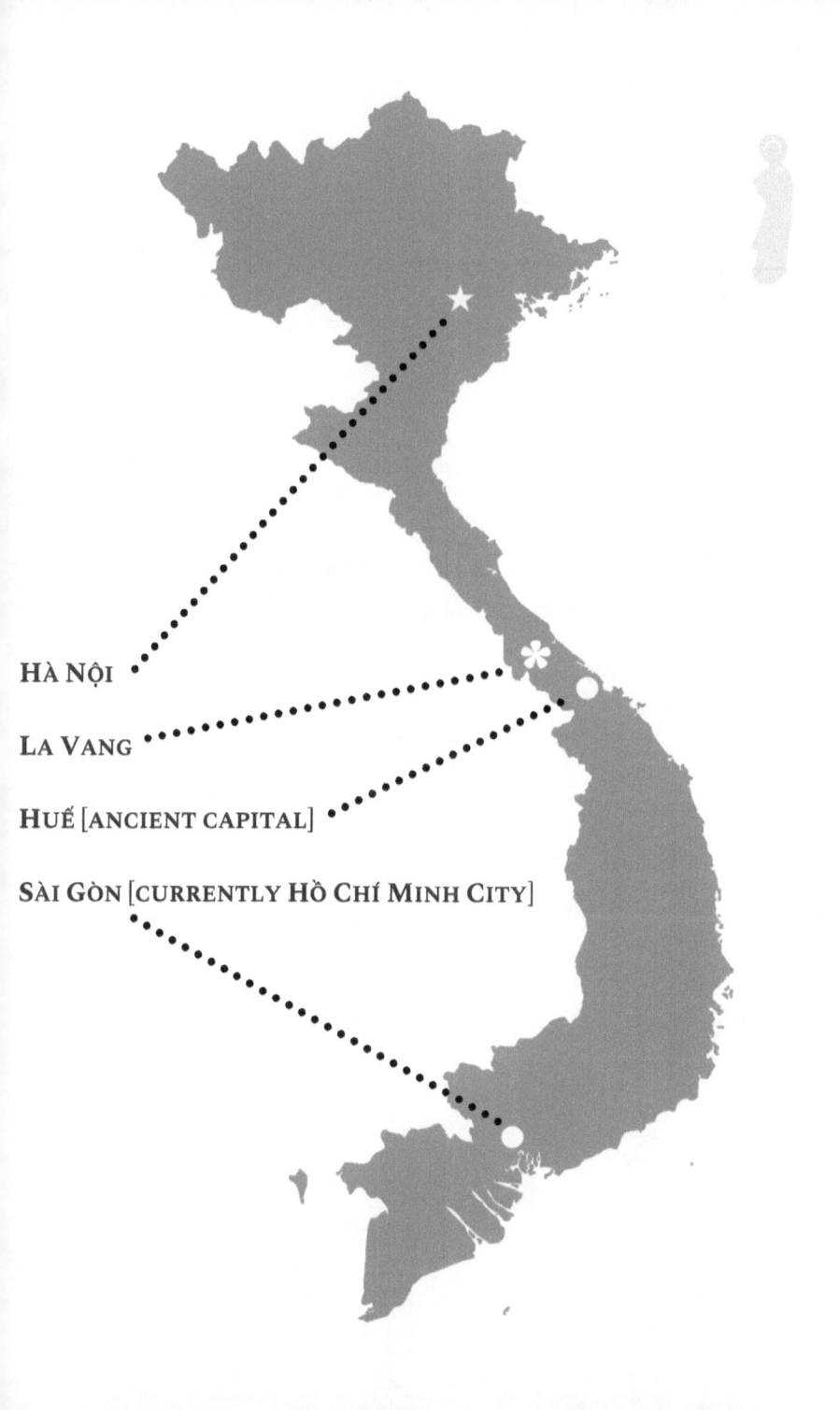

HÀ NỘI

LA VANG

HUẾ [ANCIENT CAPITAL]

SÀI GÒN [CURRENTLY HỒ CHÍ MINH CITY]

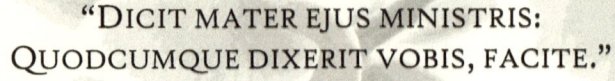

"Dicit mater ejus ministris:
Quodcumque dixerit vobis, facite."

John 2:5

LITTLE LAN

I We went where no one went.

Even our hunters never went that far. Anyone who did never returned.

I remember my brothers and my father shared stories of the jungle's darkness: how it dimmed their eyes in the day, smothered their torches at night, and even made full moons shy away.

"Remember! You must see with your ears and nose. Your eyes will deceive in the jungle." Father said to Anh Vinh.[1] I watched as they prepared for their next hunt – sharpening their arrows and knives, the metal scraping against stone, the subtle iron wafting like a fresh rain. It was my favorite smell.

"Bố, tell me the story when you found the tigers," I asked my father.[2] He did not stop sharpening, but said,

---

[1] *Anh Vinh*, pronounced as spelled, with *anh* meaning *elder brother*, *Vinh* as a proper masculine name.

[2] *Bố*, pronounced roughly "boh", meaning *dad* with a casual intimacy. During this time period, children commonly addressed their fathers as *Thầy*, meaning *Teacher*, emphasizing their duty to instruct the family. This novel features modern terms, rather than

"We did not find the tigers – they found us. You heard the story many times, Con.[3] Why do you like it so much?"

"I want to know how to stop them from finding me."

Bố and Anh Vinh laughed, but I was serious. "They found us because they smelled the blood of your brother's boar. The mother was teaching her cubs, and when they saw us instead, they stared until they ran away."

"We scared them because they never saw men before." Anh explained. It was the deepest they ever went in the jungle. "But we don't know if they will stay scared, so we will not return there."

Since I had never seen one, I imagined how they looked while Bố described them, "they have fiery fur, amber and white like embers, between black smears like coal stains. Around the mouth is a white beard, and their eyes glow gold."

The village bell sounded and erased my drawing of the tigers. It was time for us to remember when the Angel visited the Queen. I tried to keep up with Bố and Anh, but the words were still strange, and I worried about kneeling at the right time – *et habitavit in nobis*.[4]

---

historically accurate terms, to aid in learning today's Việtnamese.

[3] Pronounced "gon", meaning *child* and may be used as a pronoun referring to a child.

[4] Meaning "and dwelt among us", referring to the Incarnation of Christ, memorialized in the Prayer of the Angelus, from John 1:14.

When we finished, Mẹ called us to lunch.[5] She made our family favorite, and my brothers and I fought over the savory eggs like we always did. I almost choked on the sweetly sauced rice, like I always did. "Eat slowly. Sons, have more of the boar. Maybe it will help you hunt another one today," she said, "let your little sister have the last egg."

"Lan, I'll trade you the egg for the first wild orchid I find during the hunt."[6] Anh Vinh promised.

"They're not even blooming right now." I said.

"Fine, some other wild flower, then?"

I bit the egg as my answer – I knew he would still bring me a flower.

"The rainy season is nearing. Maybe sooner this year." Bố said, "Khoa, have you checked your traps?"[7] My other brother, between Anh Vinh and me, looked up from his bowl of soup. He had been setting improvised snares in hopes of catching even more this season.

"Not yet, Bố. Still too soon, I think," then Anh Khoa looked at me, "and stay away from the sầu riêng trap – do you hear, Lan?" I remember how he had wrapped durian[8]

---

[5] *Mẹ*, pronounced roughly "meah" ("yeah" with M instead of Y), meaning *mom, mother*.

[6] *Lan*, pronounced like the "Lan" in *"Milan or Mulan"*, a proper feminine name meaning *orchid flower*.

[7] *Khoa*, pronounced "kwah", a proper masculine name.

[8] Durian (*sầu riêng*, pronounced roughly "sau reeng") are melon-sized tropical fruit with a protective rind of tough sharp spikes,

husks around a bamboo stalk, very carefully avoiding the needle-pointed spikes. It looked like a turtle shell covered with spear tips. He had pulled the stalk back, shivering against the bamboo's tension until he tied the rope down onto a twig. The turtle disappeared under leaves and shadows.

"I know, I know… it's very dangerous." I sighed. I scratched the dirt floor with my fingers, drawing a durian fruit with feet. It looked like a fearsome turtle.

When we finished eating, the village bell rang out.

But it was too soon.

We just finished an Angelus, and Mass was earlier.

I remember we all looked at each other, yet the bell kept rousing every ear near enough.

The bell was screaming.

Bố beckoned us to follow him outside, and all around us people came out of their huts, going to the chapel. As we approached, the damp ground was pockmarked with hoof prints and shoeprints. I wanted to stare at the strange intricate patterns, but we all hurried before the bell stopped. Somehow, we knew we needed to be present before it stopped, and we knew it was not Cha who was ringing it. [9]

---

and considered a sweet delicacy with a powerfully pungent odor. In Asia, it is often banned in public places due to its smell; some people love it, others have perpetual enmity with it.

[9] *Cha,* pronounced "jah", meaning *father*, used as a formal address, but also used when casually referring to a Catholic priest.

The Edict

2 A young soldier on horseback struck the bell until the mandarin raised his hand.[10] We waited for the mandarin to speak – he waited for the bell to still. I wondered why he looked at us for so long, and only realized much later that he was counting us carefully.

Many moments passed before he began.

He unclasped a silk sleeve from his shoulders – the blue shimmer of cloth caught the breeze and writhed like a rushing stream. From the sleeve, he revealed a scroll tattooed with characters that looked like small burned rice scattered all over. The mandarin did not look at us as he read,[11] but I never looked away. Even with my head respectfully down, my eyes focused on him. All I could hear was the wind slapping his banners and flags, flying from the mounted horses surrounding him. They were applauding.

---

[10] *Mandarins* refer to elite government officials of some past East Asian empires, especially China and Việtnam. The bureaucratic organization of dynastic rule made highly skilled mandarins essential.

[11] See Appendix for an example of an anti-Christian Imperial Việtnamese edict from 1833.

I started listening when a whip cracked the bamboo hat off my neighbor's head.

"We plainly see your hearts have been darkened from following this foreign influence. You do not even greet your officials with kowtows or gifts," the mandarin said in a very even voice. The split hat dusted the ground in the wind.

Cha spoke as he came forward. He stepped between me and the mandarin – his tattered cassock was like a shadow blocking my view. "Forgive me, your honor, but we pray for the Emperor and all of you every day. Our prayers to Chúa Giêsu Kitô[12] are worth more than all kowtows or gifts we can give." Cha's calm voice reminded me of his chants – he always sounded like he was praying.

"Linh Mục Roux, we will accept you as a gift of a departing guest to our Empire."[13] The mandarin poked Cha's face with the scroll. "You and this village have until first light tomorrow to revert this shack into a shrine for the Emperor. Afterwards, you will offer prayers *to* him and our ancestors, not *for* him."

The soldiers followed the mandarin as he turned away and left. The soldier who had rung the bell was staring at me when I noticed he was the last one to leave. He did not look any older than my own brothers.

---

[12] Pronounced roughly "Juah Yeh-soo Gee-doh", meaning *Lord (Chúa) Jesus (Giêsu) Christ (Kitô)*.
[13] *Linh Mục*, pronounced roughly "Lin Mook", a formal way of addressing a priest, meaning *reverend*, or *clergyman/cleric*.

We watched and waited for Cha to speak, but he only went into the chapel. His cassock disappeared into the dark doorway. My parents followed, and we all followed.

Inside, Cha was lighting the skinny candles – they looked like golden chopsticks around the altar. My brothers robed themselves in cassocks and helped Cha light the joss sticks – the smell and smoke swirled as they walked through.

My big sister and her young family knelt beside us, and she draped a veil over my hair, "Lan, did you forget yours again?" she whispered as she nudged me. Mẹ nodded as Chị Vy[14] tugged out another veil for her also, but from the edge of mine, I could see Bố whispering words with his forehead on the floor. Everyone around me started doing the same with knotted cords between their fingers.

"My children," Cha Roux started, his vestments shimmering in the candlelight, "we will pray this Holy Mass for the Emperor's conversion and that of all his mandarins, soldiers, and servants. Afterwards, I will adore Chúa here until sunrise. You are all welcome to join me in silence or song as we keep vigil." Then Cha turned east and began, "*In Nomine Patris, et Filii, et Spiritus Sancti. Amen. Introibo ad altare Dei....*"[15]

---

[14] Pronounced roughly "Jee Vee", with *chị* meaning *elder sister*, *Vy* as a proper feminine name.

[15] The beginning words of the priest at the Traditional Roman Catholic Mass, commencing with the *Prayers at the Foot of the*

THE LAST NIGHT

3 The choir of crickets outside masked our voices as Cha heard our sins into dusk. I remember watching the candlesticks shrink and the wax trap moths that flew too close – it distracted me as the adults started going out to talk. Although they were too far for me to hear well, I could tell they were upset.

"Anh Vinh, do you know what's happening?"

My brother was peeking through the wall slats and beckoned me over. That was when I saw our neighbors: some were trying to bring their old ancestral shrine tablets to the chapel, others were blocking them, "Is your faith so small? Get these idols away!"

"We must at least disguise the chapel, or else they will destroy it."

"But if we do this, destroying the chapel would make no difference. It would only reflect self-destroyed faith."

Altar. Before 1970, the Mass was said entirely in the holy language of Latin (with some Greek and Hebrew), and the rubrics and prayers of Holy Mass originated from before the canon of the New Testament was even established. The modern Novus Ordo Mass since 1970 has lost many ancient elements. For much more information, see LatinMass.com.

The adults fought back and forth.

Back and forth until Cha approached, whispered, and collected the teak tablets, each engraved with the names of our ancestors. Those he could not carry, the rest of the villagers brought into the chapel and lined them along the foot of the altar and the walls.

"My beloved children," Cha explained, "it is not good that we be alone. We must pray with all our ancestors. Let us invite them to join us in our vigil with our Lord and Lady." With that, the entire village soon crowded the candlelit chapel with us, with long-lost family, and with hymns and chants. Although we were all tired, I remember no one falling asleep. It reminded me of the time when Cha shared the story of the Apostle preaching in the upper room, speaking late into the night – speaking so much, and so long, that a young man who sat on a window ledge fell fast asleep and fell fast to the ground! Dead! I can still hear Cha telling the tale:

And then Saint Paul stopped when everyone in the room gasped at the loud scream and thud out below. The young man's family must've shrieked! Then Saint Paul must've rushed down, wishing that he himself had fallen out instead. But imagine the shock of all when he raised the boy up back to life... refreshed from the nap! But do not worry, my children, since I cannot raise anyone back to life, I will never preach as long as that. You are safe. Cha had snickered.[16]

---

[16] Cha is retelling Acts 20:7-12.

"We are safe," Mẹ said to me as I leaned against her bosom, "you can sleep, Con. Mẹ will say your prayers for you." I listened to Mother's heart sing its lullaby, and I thought I could hear my baby sibling's own heart from deeper inside.

I dreamed about him or her: if he would be like Anh Vinh or Anh Khoa – or would she be like Chị and me?

Both Bloods

4 I woke when the bell rang for Cha to raise up the Body – it glowed like a little full moon. The shimmer of the Chalice was the first light in my eyes. Sunrise glanced off it from between Cha's fingertips. He always cradled it like a little bird nest resting safely atop bamboo branches.[17]

Then the Chalice sprung from its cradle, smeared with Cha's blood and the Precious Blood. The gold rung louder than the bell as it banged off the wall and onto the floor. An arrow bit into the window frame above the altar, and Cha's fingers dangled from his hands. His white surplice was instantly embroidered with both bloods. The little moons floated up and fluttered around like falling leaves.

I saw the Chalice's face sunken in with a deep scar from the arrowhead. It rolled on the wood floor, circling itself within a red halo. Mẹ held me close as the soldiers

---

[17] Before 1970, priests celebrated Holy Mass facing *ad orientem* (*to the East*, in anticipation of Christ's return), and at the proper times, elevated the Host and Chalice high above their heads, as high as they could reach, for all to see our Lord raised up.

rushed inside and pushed us all apart. Cha fell to his knees, his mangled hands gripped the altar's edge, and he leaned up to kiss and take the Body.

The soldiers grabbed and dragged Cha past us. I heard him whisper "*Pater, dimitte illis: non enim sciunt...*"[18] He had said that often.

The soldiers did not need to make us – we all came out to see the mandarin, and I saw the young soldier with his bow still in hand.

"Chào Linh Mục Roux,"[19] the mandarin said as the soldiers brought Cha forward like a puppet. My brothers were brought out with him, "Chào các con," [20] the mandarin said, looking down at Anh Khoa and Anh Vinh who still grasped the giant teak crucifix. Cha had carved it for parades and processions, and it was half my size.

"Please, your honor..." a villager spoke up, I could not tell who because she was sobbing, "please see for yourself that the chapel... is now as you wished."

The mandarin continued staring at my brothers, but said, "Is it? Then how is it that you were having your Christian ritual within just now?" The mandarin walked his horse through the crowd straight to the old woman. It was Bà Nhi,[21] the eldest grandmother of the village.

---

[18] Luke 23:34, *Father, forgive them: they do not know...*

[19] *Chào*, pronounced roughly "jao", meaning *hello*.

[20] *Các*, pronounced roughly "gahk", meaning *each, all,* or *every*.

[21] *Bà Nhi*, pronounced roughly "Bah Nyee", with *Bà* meaning *elderly woman, grandmother; Nhi* as a proper feminine name.

"But if you are speaking truthfully, then I thank you for being a good example to all the youth of your village. Please, be first then to prove your genuine return to our culture and religion." The mandarin beckoned Bà to follow him – he led her before Cha. The soldiers kicked the back of his knees and flattened him to the ground. His vestments furled up as he fell like a bright cloud. The soldiers tore away the vestments.

The mandarin dismounted his horse and stepped on Cha's face.

He commanded and waited for Bà to do the same.

She hung her head and trembled.

She would not.

"Con ơi,"[22] Cha said, his voice rough, "I am nothing. Do not fear what you must do."

But she would not.

The mandarin shook his head, "So then... you sought to deceive me, after all. Your age has only increased your insolence. Your disgraceful example must be dealt with, you understand?"

"Please, Con," Cha pleaded with Bà. It was the only time I ever heard him cry out, "... you must."

"Anything done now would merely be deceit." The mandarin returned to my brothers. Anh Vinh embraced the crucifix across his chest. "I am an extension of the

---

[22] *Ơi*, pronounced roughly "uh-ee", a term used to soften a tone, or also add endearment to a name or pronoun.

Emperor, and his benevolent wisdom understands you may find trampling a man's face to be dishonorable, despite the imperial command." The mandarin wrenched the crucifix from Anh Vinh and dropped it beside Cha's head, "You may use this as a stepping stone onto Linh Mục Roux."

Everyone, everything stood still.

The mandarin waited for Bà.

We all waited.

I remember Mother's heart stopped.

Anh Vinh had dashed forward, snatched the crucifix, and bolted for the forest.

Everyone, everything went everywhere.

THE CAVE

5 The young soldier drew an arrow and aimed. The sound of the bowstring and arrow screamed as it chased Anh.

It caught someone else instead, "Chạy, Con! Chạy!"[23] Bố shouted.

My hand was suddenly in Anh Khoa's, and Mẹ threw me into his arms. She kissed us off before rushing to Bố's side. Dust and tears stained my view, so I never knew until later if they had spent their last moments together.

Brother ran, carrying me away from the struggle between the village and the soldiers, "Em, are you injured?"[24] He asked me, but I could not answer. My breaths filled with water – it felt like drowning even though the wind blew.

Once I could wipe my eyes, we were somehow already in our cave. It was not far from the treeline, and we had left many things there. My brothers and I used it to play for many years.

---

[23] Pronounced roughly "jay", meaning *run*.
[24] *Em*, pronounced "am", meaning *younger sibling*, but also refers to anyone younger within one's own generation.

Anh Khoa just held me as we sat in the darkness. The mouth of the cave was a bright green circle of leaves lit by daylight. I tried not to cry out when a black shadow came into view and smothered the circle like a growing inkblot.

When I saw Anh Vinh, he held a flower up to my eyes. I grabbed him and sobbed, but he kept trying to show the flower to me, "Lan ơi, coi đây!"[25] I shook my head in his chest. I did not care about flowers.

"It's an orchid! And they're not in bloom!" Anh told me, "as you said!"

"Where did you find it?" Anh Khoa asked.

"On the way here. Kỳ lạ..."[26]

"It may be a trap."

"You see a trap in everything," Anh Vinh sighed, "but still, how would anyone get orchids anywhere now?

"I don't know, but I know we can't stay here for long. This cave is not hard to find." Anh Khoa started collecting things we stashed in the dark.

"I thought of that already. We can stay hidden longer. Help me." Anh Vinh said, placing his crucifix on a rock. My brothers snuck to the cave's mouth. I watched them drape vines and branches over the green circle, slowly, carefully, quietly masking a giant's yawn. I picked up Anh Vinh's crucifix and held it to my heart, praying in

---

[25] *Coi đây*, pronounced "goy day", meaning *look here*.

[26] *Kỳ lạ*, pronounced roughly "gee lah", meaning *strange, weird*.

whispers for Cha, Bố, Mẹ, Chị, and hai Anh. [27] I remembered and added Bà and everyone who disappeared in the swarm of soldiers, "*Ave Maria, gratia plena, Dominus tecum...*"[28]

It was the first time I prayed with my whole heart.

"Em ơi," Anh Khoa called to me, "do you need anything? Are you thirsty?"

I said no, even though I was, because I did not want him to go away.

"Anh Vinh went to get his bow and find food, I'll be back with water. It will be too cold tonight without eating."

"Please don't leave me..."

"We'll be back soon. Just stay in here with your guardian angel." Anh picked up the orchid from my lap and set it in my hair before he left.

I continued my Rosary, counting with a cord of knots wrapped around my wrist.

I prayed until I fell asleep, my head resting on the arm of the crucifix.

In my dream, I saw orchids springing up in the jungle, a trail of blossoms leading me deeper. A huge banyan tree with legs like a hundred jellyfish glowed with a headdress of branches in moonlight. Between the tree's legs were many rooms, prepared for all of us.

---

[27] *Hai*, pronounced "hye", meaning *two*, or *both*.

[28] *Hail Mary, full of grace, the Lord is with thee...*, from Luke 1:28.

Then the moon emerged from the tree's crown, and I saw the little moons again. He was all alone on the chapel floor.

His lonesome heartache woke me.

I set the crucifix on a flat stone, nestled the orchid flower beside His crown of thorns, and left the cave to find Him.

MINI MOONS

6 The village was empty while I watched it from the treeline. I watched it for a long time, until even the sun started to stop watching.

No one was left.

I listened and heard not a voice or cough, not even a footstep or cockcrow. After seeing and hearing nothing, I waited until sundown before I crouched and crawled back to the chapel. Dusk hid me while I searched the ground around where Cha had been kicked down, and where the crucifix left its imprint. I saw the place where Cha's loosed fingers had clenched the dirt, and where Bố had fallen. It was a dried and stained patch of muddy blood.

I knelt where Mẹ would have – I touched the stain and added teardrops to it. I picked up some of the stained grains and carried them in my palms.

Inside the chapel, the ancestral tablets were shattered and scattered, along with the statues of our Queen and her Son. I tiptoed around, over the rubble, and found the little moons – dozens.

After placing the stained grains at the altar, I stooped down before the many moons, "*Meus Deus, meus*

Dominus,[29] lạy Chúa ơi please have mercy on Bố Mẹ, on Chị and her family, and hai Anh... let us be together again."[30]

I leaned down, kowtowed,[31] whispered, "*Domine non sum dignus, ut intres sub tectum meum, sed tantum dic verbo et sanabitur anima mea*,"[32] and pressed my lips to a moon, kissing Him as did the woman who had washed His feet with her hair and tears. Walking on my knees to another moon, I leaned down and prayed the same again, kissing Him again – and again.

Until the small full moons had all become new moons.

After my supper with my King, I noticed one of my brothers at the chapel's doorway. I had wondered if they would find me. He watched, but I did not care. He came beside me, "Em ơi..."

I jumped away.

It was not my brother.

"Em ơi, please don't be afraid."

In the twilight, I could barely see, but it was the young soldier.

---

[29] *My God, my Lord*, echoing St. Thomas the Apostle in John 20:28.
[30] *Lạy Chúa*, pronounced roughly "ley Juah" meaning *Oh Lord God*.
[31] *Kowtowing* means to kneel and lean forward until one's forehead contacts the ground. It is an act showing humility, subordination, and worship, common in some East Asian cultures.
[32] A prayer of the Roman Catholic Mass that paraphrases and echoes the soldier of Matthew 8:8.

THE TRAPS

7 I stared at him.

He stepped back from me with a limp, careful not to come nearer.

You killed Bố. You shot Cha. You almost killed Anh Vinh.

"Please em, I will not harm you."

I glared at him.

You already did.

The setting sun disappeared as I noticed his left leg was shredded. I grabbed a broken tablet and clenched it tight. It flew from my hand as I snatched up another. He dodged the first, blocked the second, but took the third to his bloodied leg. He collapsed into the wall and dragged himself out of the smashed stones.

I got up to run out the door.

"I know about your cave!" He shouted.

I stopped.

I grabbed a broken bamboo pole. I needed to kill him.

"Go ahead, em. I know you cannot let me go now," he said as I cautiously neared, "but I just want to say I am sorry. Please forgive me."

Pater, dimitte illis: non enim sciunt...

I heard Cha.

I backed away from the soldier.

My grip trembled with the stick. I smacked the air, "You better not be lying to me!" I cried. He looked at me with a peace that did not make sense.

"My name is Đặng Lực Khang,"[33] he said, with a peace that did not make sense, "I served the high mandarin of our Emperor."

Served?

"But today, I was abandoned by my fellow imperial soldiers, and by the very mandarin I served faithfully since childhood." He looked at his wounded leg, "when I was ordered to pursue the young man who ran into the forest, I came across a trap that snared my leg in a bundle of durian husks. The more I pulled away, the more the spikes chewed into my flesh."

Anh Khoa would have smiled.

"When I laid there, unable to move from the pain, I was sure my brother soldiers would help, but the mandarin ordered them to leave me for dead. I would be too much to care for, he had said. I then listened as they rounded up your village, and marched off. They left me."

---

[33] Pronounced roughly "Dahng Luhk Kahng", a proper name.

I could see his greatest pain was not from his leg.

"Nobody is here. You are safe from the mandarin – and from me. I will not hurt you, I promise." He removed his quiver and bow and offered them to me, holding them out like they were a baby in swaddling clothes.

I took the quiver but left him the bow.

"Wait here, I'll bring water and food." I said, with a peace that surprised me. He thanked me as I bowed to the altar and slipped out into the night.

The village's quiet frightened me, and I had never seen it so dark. When I found our home, I could tell it was ours because my feet remembered the way and the steps, not because I could see. Inside, I searched the kitchen and found dried bananas and thanh long.[34] They were my favorite snacks, and we had saved some from Mother's last batch and recent harvest.

Anh Vinh found me there.

"Lan! What are you doing! You scared us gần chết!"[35]

---

[34] Pronounced roughly "tun long", meaning *dragon fruit*, a tropical fruit with a bright, pink, velvety rind, and extremely juicy white flesh inside (like watermelon), scattered with small edible black seeds (similar to kiwi seeds). Dragon fruit actually originated from South and Central America, known as *pitaya*, and was introduced to Việt Nam by French colonial influence in the mid-1800s. Yellow and red varieties exist with differing sweetness levels. Though out of place historically for this story, I wanted to include it since Việt Nam today is the leading global grower and exporter of the highly sought fruit.

[35] Pronounced roughly "gun jet", meaning *nearly to death*.

"Where's Anh Khoa?" I asked.

"At the cave, we looked all over for you. Why are you here?" Anh Vinh set down his bow, held me and checked me for wounds, "and how do you have this quiver?"

"I am fine. I came back to consume the Hosts. We left Him."

Anh Vinh picked me up and kissed me, "You are so holy and faithful. Our little saint! But we must go now. They may come back to find us."

"No, we can't go yet. I must show you something."

"Thôi! Cái gì vậy?"[36] Anh was getting impatient.

"Anh Khoa's trap caught something..."

---

[36] Pronounced roughly "Toy! Gai zee vay?", meaning *Forget it! What is it [now]?*

THE YOUNG SOLDIER

8 Anh Vinh drew his dagger when he saw the young soldier. I had told him not to worry, but he did not believe me.

"Lan ơi, this is a trick!" Anh shouted a whisper into my ear.

"Anh, remember what Cha always said and taught? *Pater, dimitte illis: non enim sciunt!*"

I could tell this made Anh even angrier, and confused the soldier.

"But he just wants us to show where any other survivors are! It's a trap!"

"*Now* who sees a trap in everything?" I teased, but it annoyed Anh.

"You have it backwards, Anh. I can show *you* where the other survivors are," the soldier said, finally. "They will be left to live until they fail to apostatize before the Emperor. Then, the mandarin will make a public example of them."

Anh and I stared at him.

"That can still be a trap, to have us captured with the rest." I admitted.

"Exactly, em," Anh set down some of the bananas and dragon fruits, "we will leave these for you, but you will not see us again." Anh Vinh pointed his dagger at the soldier.

"He knows about the cave." I said.

"How?" Anh Vinh shook the dagger, "tell us how or you die now, forgiveness or not!"

From the folds in his uniform, the soldier pulled out a fresh flower, "I followed these."

THE ORCHIDS

9 Anh Vinh and I stared at the orchid in the failing light. Though it was dark, we could see it was exactly like the one Anh had picked and given to me. Its white petals glowed a faint blue.

"Wait, but if you knew about the cave, then that could be the same flower I left there!" I shouted.

"There are many in the forest." The soldier said.

"How many? Five? Fifty?" Anh interrogated.

"Too many to be natural. They are not even in season," the soldier held out the bloom to us, "I saw the entire forest floor covered."

Anh quieted – I could tell he knew the soldier was being honest. And I could tell he hated it. The soldier offered his bow to Anh, and pointed to the quiver around my shoulder, "I surrender my arms, see I mean you no harm."

"We are leaving. You will not see us again." Anh said, taking my hand and walking away. I did not look back either, but when we came to the treeline, a patch of wild orchids stopped us.

They were not there even minutes ago.

"Anh, what does this mean?" I said as he pulled me into the new garden, trampling the blossoms. He did not answer as we returned to the cave. I had hoped Anh Khoa would be there, but he met us along the way with a small torch.

"The cave is gone." Anh Khoa said, with a strange blank face.

Anh Vinh did not believe him and pressed on. I followed closely, leaving Anh Khoa to chase us half-heartedly. It confused me why he was not scared, and why Anh Vinh was not either.

As we caught up with Anh Vinh, he stood at the cave's mouth, and we all stared at it with shock.

It was filled with orchids.

The entire cave was stuffed like a bánh chưng.[37]

"Chúa is telling us something." Anh Khoa said when he caught up, "I went out to collect firewood after you went to find Lan. I came back and found the cave full of them. I started to follow the trail of orchids when I ran into you."

Anh Vinh hesitated to touch the flowers, cautiously placing his hand on them like they were flames. He pressed against them with his palm, but they did not make way. I tried the same and the soft petals pushed

---

[37] Pronounced roughly "bun jung", meaning a boiled, dense and hefty Vietnamese glutinous rice cake wrapped in banana leaves and filled with spiced pork and mung beans. It is a holiday dish eaten only during Tết, the Vietnamese Lunar New Year.

back like a firm pillow of duckling feathers. I remembered the ducks we raised since I was even smaller.

"We should see where they lead..." Anh Vinh said, beckoning Anh Khoa to lead the way. We tracked the orchid trail back to the village.

It led to the chapel.

It led up the steps.

It led inside.

It led to the young soldier.

He was asleep when we found him, and blossoms surrounded him like a bed. The lone flower he had held out to us was now one of thousands.

"Phép lạ,"[38] Anh Vinh said. Anh Khoa's torchlight illumined the bouquets that lined the altar and embraced where I had placed Cha and Bố's grains. Flowers had also sprung from where each Host had been – I noticed those were speckled with red dots.

We shared with Anh Khoa what we knew about the soldier.

"You think it's safe to stay here tonight?" Anh Khoa asked.

Anh Vinh sighed as he sat down upon a pillow of orchid blooms, "there are four flowerbeds here... I guess one meant for each of us." He motioned me to have the one nearest the altar, furthest from the doorway.

---

[38] Pronounced roughly "făp lah", meaning *miracle* or *miraculous*.

We sat each on our own bed, silently watching the soldier sleep, watching until the torch burned out, until we all drifted off as well. I thought about my dream from earlier, and knew we were cared for.

THE FLYING FLOWER

10 Sunlight streamed through between the wood panels, hanging like sheets of sun in the dust. I remember waking and hoping to see the orchid bouquets in their full color, but when I rubbed and opened my eyes, they were all gone. I squinted my eyes, thinking I was not seeing clearly.

"Where did they all go?" Anh Khoa asked in shock. He shook Anh Vinh awake. The soldier was groggy. Anh patted the floor where flowerbeds were just hours before, but there was only the sound of his hand slapping wood. We all patted the floor in disbelief.

That was when we noticed the only blossom left was in the middle of the chapel. Anh Vinh went up to it, we followed, and I remember seeing how its stems reached out from the wood, growing from it no matter how impossible that was.

"There's another!" The soldier shouted, pointing to the doorway. The flower's lonesome silhouette fluttered in the breeze, waving at us until the wind picked it up and carried it off. I gave chase while hai Anh helped the soldier up.

My bare feet kicked up dust that whipped past me as I ran after the orchid. My heart tumbled in my chest; I don't remember ever running that fast before – that scared of losing sight of the flying flower.

It led me into the forest, took turns around Anh Khoa's traps, twisted around pits and boulders, and rested in a clearing. When the boys caught up, we watched the orchid whither into a white dust and float away like ashes. I kneeled where it was last and wanted to cry.

"Em ơi, don't cry." Anh Vinh left Anh Khoa with the soldier and came to kneel with me. I copied his Sign of the Cross and prayed with his words: "Lạy Mẹ Chúa Giêsu Kitô,[39] you led us here with these miraculous flowers. Please help us continue to follow your Son, however you will lead us. Amen."

"Amen." I said, and Anh Khoa added.

"Amen," said the soldier.

We all turned to look at him.

"You dare to pray?" Anh Vinh said.

"Against the edict's command?" Anh Khoa challenged.

"I have seen enough miracles to show me who the true Emperor is." The soldier admitted. "I know it must be difficult to trust me; I do not blame you. I thank you for trying, and I hope to earn your trust."

---

[39] Pronounced roughly "Ley Meah Juah Yeh-soo Gee-doh", meaning *Oh Mother of the Lord Jesus Christ*.

Anh Vinh tossed the soldier's bow off his shoulder, "will you keep your promise to help free our village?"

The soldier bowed, "I will. I will die trying."

"Then start." Anh Khoa said, helping the soldier to his feet. His blood-crusted leg reminded me of Simon helping our King with His cross. They limped forward – Anh Vinh and I followed.

THE PRISON CAMP

I I We walked the entire day, somehow without needing rest. Perhaps because we were eager to see our family, or perhaps we were anxious of the soldier betraying us, or maybe it was all another miracle. When we neared the camp, it was dusk again, but the soldier hid us where he knew the sentinels could not see.

"Should we wait here until first light?" Anh Khoa asked.

"No need, I know the way well, even in the dark." The soldier started to crawl, and his leg became coated in mud as he dragged it like a tail.

The darkening jungle revealed torches lit in the distance. The soldier pointed to them with his head, and we followed without a word until he swept aside some branches to show the view ahead and below: it was our village, but instead of homes and a chapel, it was cages and barracks.

We watched from atop a hill for a very long time.

Then a shadow we recognized appeared.

They dragged Cha from a cramped bamboo cage too small for his size. I imagined how he must have been folded, twisted, and forced to fit inside.

I covered my mouth before I could cry out to him. We watched the soldiers bring him to the seated mandarin, surrounded by torches in the night, and surrounded by people from our village and others. Men and boys sat in cages to the left, women and girls in cages to the right. The mandarin's voice was faint, but we could hear. Somehow, even the crickets and mosquitos went silent when he spoke.

"Linh Mục Roux, we will now accept you as your parting gift to the Emperor. If you truly revere him, simply place him above your Giêsu Kitô. Do so as a good example for your so-called flock." The mandarin gestured to a pole with two images on the ground before it: one was Mẹ Maria and Her Son, the other was the Emperor's portrait.

The mandarin waited, but Cha did not move.

We also waited, and did not move.

I do not think I even breathed.

Finally, the mandarin hung up the icon, "There, I did the first step for you. Now simply raise the Emperor's image to his rightful place." He swept his long silk-sleeved arms from Cha towards the portrait.

Cha was motionless as an island at sea.

Everyone sat in their cages like stumps and lumps.

The mandarin just watched, just as unmoving. His sleeves and robe swayed in the wind.

When the mandarin turned away, soldiers emerged from the darkness like ghosts, snatched Cha, and melted his shadow into theirs. They dropped him at the edge of the camp beside a post, tied him there by his ankles and wrists, and left him kneeling on mats of durian shells. We could smell the fruit's rotten rinds. They were one of my favorite fruits, but I hated them being used this way.

"Your Cha will be a good example for you, one way or another," the mandarin proclaimed, "by the end of these three days, we shall see if he can be raised from the dead."

Tears blurred my vision, especially when Anh Vinh asked if we saw Bố Mẹ[40] anywhere. I began to tremble remembering when I last saw them.

Then Anh Khoa said he saw Chị Vy.
I wiped my eyes as he pointed her out to me. I knew the slope of her hair on her head – it was much like mine, Mẹ always said. Chị was years older than us, but she had always been like my twin. We laughed and joked that someday, even my own future husband and children would look like hers.

"Time to leave." The soldier suddenly said.

"What?" We resisted – shocked.

---

[40] Listing pairs this way is common and acceptable in Việtnamese, without a comma or conjunction. Here, both *Father Mother* are listed.

"There is nothing we can do tonight," the soldier said, "we will return tomorrow. We just needed to know who was left, and where they are exactly."

"What do you mean? We are freeing them right now!" Anh Khoa said.

"No it would be too obvious and dangerous if –"

"Now." Anh Vinh said.

The soldier hesitated.

"*Now* – or we leave you with the mandarin, *for dead* as a traitor.*" I said.

The soldier and hai Anh glanced at me.

He gave a nod.

We started following the soldier away from the camp when we heard chanting:

> *Salve Regina,*
> *Mater misericordiæ,*
> *vita dulcedo et spes nostra, salve...*[41]

---

[41] The beginning of the *Hail Holy Queen* chanted in Latin, and continued in the next chapter.

SINGING AND SINGEING

12 My lips started joining the *Salve* on their own.
"Come, we must keep going." The soldier said – I could tell he knew what would happen next. He grabbed my arm.

Anh Vinh grabbed him.

Anh Khoa shoved him.

"Never touch our sister."

> *Ad te clamamus...*
> *exsules filii Hevæ...*
> *ad te suspiramus,*
> *gementes et flentes...*
> *in hac lacrimarum valle...*

Then screams joined in.

I heard Chị cry out – even our cries sounded alike. I knew hai Anh heard her also.

"What's happening!" Anh Khoa rushed back to see.

Anh Vinh shook the soldier for answers.

I watched from beside Anh Khoa, heard the soldier describe exactly what we saw: "The Emperor considers

Christians as followers of a perverse religion. To warn others off from converting, the Emperor has mandated all obstinate Christians shamefully branded with 左道 upon their cheeks, each character on its own cheek."[42]

Eia ergo...
advocata nostra...
illos tuos... misericordes... oculos...
ad nos converte...

Soldiers held Chị down as she squirmed from the raw pain on her left cheek. I could see her tears shining in the torchlight, and shining from the raised molten brand nearing her right cheek. A soldier gripped her hair and steadied her face, baring her cheek for the red metal 道. All the while, Chị kept singing in a breaking voice:

Et Iesum...
benedictum fructum... ventris tui...
nobis... post hoc exsilium... ostende...

---

[42] 左道, pronounced roughly in Cantonese Chinese "jaw doe", in Mandarin Chinese Pinyin "zuǒ dào", in Việtnamese *Tả Đạo*, pronounced roughly: "da dao", meaning *left (perverse) religion/direction*. Many East Asian cultures superstitiously regarded the left of anything (left hand, left side, etc.) to be wayward and corrupted, not unlike the English language's word for *sinister* originating from the Latin word for *left*.

The brand flew from the soldier's hand with a sharp clang, like two swords meeting in battle. The sound ended everyone's singing – and breathing.

The straw roof of a barrack caught the glowing brand. It bounced and sat like a red egg on a nest. Fire hatched from it. A phoenix flew forth and began eating the barracks whole.

The camp flashed into daylight from the blaze.

Hai Anh and I turned around to see the soldier holding his empty bow with a vibrating string. I remember his eyes fixed past us into the blaze.

"Chạy mau!"[43] He shouted, watching his brother soldiers nock, aim, and fire their arrows. He shot them before some could even draw. The jungle's darkness hid us well.

"Đặng Lực Khang!" A voice called out from the camp, "you dare betray the Emperor!" The mandarin roared. "Find the traitor and bring–"

An arrow swiped the mandarin's mouth and silenced him. Blood flew out like he was vomiting. Anh Vinh drew another arrow, ready whenever the soldier was reloading.

"Khoa, get Lan somewhere safe!"

But then I saw a lone orchid down in the middle of the camp – a bright white puff in the courtyard.

Without a thought, I ran straight to it.

---

[43] *Mau*, pronounced roughly "mao", meaning *quickly, fast.*

FOLLOW THE FLOWERS

13 "Lan!" I heard my brothers shout, but I did not care. I knew we could trust the orchids. I locked my eyes onto it as I ran down the hill. It fluttered like small paper fans with the growing fire behind it. The jungle's darkness backed away from the flames. Soon, I was in the camp, and I disappeared into the mess of soldiers and villagers running in all directions.

When I found where the orchid was, it had gone. I spun in a circle, looking for it. Another had taken root nearby the cages closest to me. Guards saw me hurrying to the cages as other village girls fled, but arrows from Anh Vinh and Khang dropped the guards.

The orchid fanned out below a knot of cords just out of reach of the caged men. Flames began to creep up to them. Their arms reached for me through the bamboo grating – they called out to me, "Bé Lan, help us! Undo the knots!"[44] They were my village neighbors – I did not recognize them behind their mess of scabs and bruises.

The men had already been branded.

---

[44] *Bé*, pronounced roughly "beah" ("yeah" with B instead of Y), meaning *young child*, or *baby/infant*.

My fingers bit into the knots and started to tug them loose. Even though it was only rope, it was tight and solid as stone. No matter how much I tried, it would not give. Instead, I ran to the burning barracks, snatched a burning stick, and burned the knots apart. When they blackened and caught fire, their coils sprang apart like frightened snakes.

The cage doors surrendered as the men pushed out. I watched for Bố in the rushing crowd, hoping to see him, hoping he would hold me and bring us all home. I thought I saw him several times, but the cage emptied while I kept waiting.

Anh Khoa picked me up and carried me away. The empty cage caught fire as he brought me into the forest. Everyone was screaming, shouting, hiding, hurrying as far from the camp as possible, as fast as possible. It was strange that no soldiers were chasing anyone, but then Khang stopped us.

"We must hide. The imperial soldiers have already prepared an ambush at the perimeter. No one will escape by trying to escape." He said. We trusted him and began to climb a tree high into its crown. The vines were like ladder rungs, and as we went higher, the tree's sway rocked us gently like we were its infants.

From above, we could see a ring of torches circling the dark jungle around the camp. We caught our breaths as Khang explained to us: "The surrounding fence of soldiers was planned for such a prison break. The sentinels will secretly stand guard and shoot everyone who nears, then they will close the circle at daybreak until everyone is found – dead or alive."

I could not bear knowing the villagers were just freed only to be killed. I could not stand imagining Chị surviving and escaping, only to die with false hope. I wanted to scream – and I did.

"Follow the orchids! Everyone follow the orchids!" I cried into the sky.

I did not know if there were even any orchids for anyone to follow. I did not know if anyone else could even see them as hai Anh, Khang, and I did. I did not even know if the soldiers could also see them. I just took in a breath to scream again.

"Just follow the orchids!" Anh Vinh echoed me. All around us on the forest floor, a faint web of glowing white veins caught the moonlight and the burning camp, their paths stretching out in dozens of directions.

An arrow flew past and snipped leaves around us.

Another struck into the tree's bark.

"Xuống, xuống mau!"[45] Anh Khoa threw me onto his back and slid us down. We landed on the ground in a cushion of orchids.

---

[45] Pronounced roughly "soong", meaning *down, descend*.

43

"Lan... mày điên thật,"[46] Anh Vinh said to me, kissed me, and carried me as we chased a blooming trail into the jungle. The winding, flowering paths stretched before us in the dark, like a long white dragon soaring the night sky.[47]

---

[46] Pronounced roughly "may deen tut", meaning *you're truly insane*. *Mày*, meaning *you*, is only used informally in close relationships, and can be deeply offensive when used incorrectly.

[47] East Asian cultures see the mythical serpentine dragon as a wise and beneficent being, quite contrary to Western depictions. In some Roman Catholic churches in Chinese areas, the Asian dragon is even used in decorations to depict virtue. Through proper inculturation, I am convinced that East Asian artists could soundly use the Asian dragon to depict angels, just as Western artists chose to depict incorporeal angels as humanlike.

NIGHT HUNT

14 We were alone on the trail for a long time, and had long passed through the fence of sentinels without seeing anyone. We did not even hear anyone, but I tried my best to see with my ears and nose.

I could tell Anh Vinh was tired since Anh Khoa and the limping soldier had caught up. We stopped at a small stream for water.

"Have you noticed the orchids smell sweeter than mía?"[48] I held one up to breathe in – it filled my hungry belly somehow.

"You always had a good nose." Anh Vinh said, but shook his head, "I don't smell anything."

Anh Khoa and Khang tried to smell them, too. I wondered if they were all folded paper flowers, but they felt alive in my fingers. No one else seemed to smell their delicious aroma – I wanted to eat bouquet after bouquet.

"Do you think we'll see Bố Mẹ again? Cha? Chị and her family?"

Hai Anh did not answer.

---

[48] *Mía*, pronounced roughly "meeya", meaning *sugarcane*.

"I will go back to find them." Khang said, washing off his wounded leg downstream. He began pushing himself back onto his feet, using his bow as a cane.

"No," Anh Vinh stopped him, "you're too weak from your injuries. Wait until you recover, then I will go with you."

"I cannot risk you being captured. Your sister needs you."

"*You're* the one who will be captured, you cripple." Anh Vinh sneered.

"Stop. Let's keep moving," Anh Khoa interrupted, "this path must be leading us somewhere. If – when – and who should go back will be made clear, just as the orchids have made other things clear."

"Thank you for stopping them from branding Chị." I said to Khang. He bowed his head.

"I wish I had stopped them before the first brand."

I bowed to him in return. When I stood up straight, Anh Vinh hushed us and stared into the distance.

Something watched us from the darkness.

Khang and Anh drew their bows, and their breaths whispered into silence. Anh Khoa put me behind him and looked around us.

I tried to see what they could, hear what they heard, and smell for it.

The eyes were golden flames. Its white beard caught the moonlight.

Wind blew leaves over them, and they were gone.

"Is it hunting us?" Anh Khoa asked.

"No... we would be dead already if it was."

"Likely I smell like food." Khang admitted.

Then shouts and shrieks shot from shadows.

Men burst toward us – crawling and clawing to us.

A forest fire pounced on them.

The tiger's blazing body engulfed all the men. I could not see how many there were.

It pulled them back into the dark.

Somehow, it grew quiet again – fast.

"I knew those assassins..." Khang whispered, "they would have killed us..."

We all paused.

"Let's leave it to eat in peace..." Anh Khoa said.

Khang nodded.

"You and Lan stay between Khoa and me." Anh Vinh led us forward.

We walked on without a word between us, wondering when dawn would finally gnaw away the thick night, wondering when the orchids would fade from the trail. I kept the *Ave Maria* silently on my lips until Khang collapsed behind me.

THE BEAUTIFUL WOMAN

15 Khang did not answer whatever we asked. In the shy light of sunrise, his face was pale and greening like a guava peel. His skin was cool in our hands as we dragged him to the nearest tree – a banyan tree I thought I had seen before. Its many legs held open many lonesome rooms ready for us, like a vacant palace. An orchid grew out of its side.

"Bring him here," with a stick, I cleaned out a wide gap perfect for him to lie within. The tree's walls would hide him well.

"He needs to eat." Anh Khoa started peeling vines from the tree's legs, twisting them into cord, "can you hunt something?" He asked Anh Vinh, who was already searching the forest floor for any signs.

"Stay hidden while I'm gone."

"My traps will have their usual markings – watch for them on your way back." Anh Khoa warned Anh Vinh. With a quiet nod, Anh Vinh left pursuing boar tracks.

After finishing some lengths of rope and sharpening sticks with his dagger, Anh Khoa also left. I held a freshly carved spear in each hand while I sat with Khang, his head resting on my knees. I listened to his breaths, to my own, and to the jungle's.

I did not realize I had fallen asleep, but when I woke, I saw I had drooped over Khang, and had drooled over his face. I was so ashamed. I wiped his face with my sleeves, and looked up at the sudden sound of a sigh.

It was definitely a sigh.

One of contentment and shaped by a smile.

Then I heard footsteps, then the whisp of a sash in the breeze – though the jungle was still and suffocating.

The hem of an áo dài[49] caught my glance as I searched the dim green forest. I almost missed it when it flashed into view again. Its blue shade shimmered in a way I never saw on any silk. Not even a shining blue sky ever lit my eyes that way.

She was donned in dawn.

Her feet walked in shoes as white as the moon. Jade, rich and deep, swirled in her eyes, and her khăn đóng[50] framed her face with a halo like the gold ring of a solar eclipse. Teardrops laced her cheeks and chin like dust from gems.

---

[49] Pronounced roughly "ow zai", meaning *long gown/robe*, but refers to the traditional Việtnamese silk tunic paired with trousers, worn for festive and formal occasions alike. Male and female versions exist.

[50] Pronounced roughly "kun dong", meaning *close-looped ribbon/scarf*, but refers to the traditional Việtnamese headpiece made of offset layered fabric. The headpiece pairs with áo dài, and can mark various social positions, including royalty.

She was not any older than Chị Vy, and she held her infant Son close, whose hands and feet were pierced.

She said nothing.

But her heart sang to me.

I said nothing, but watched her reach up for the banyan's many vines, picking off little leaves. She placed and pressed them onto Khang's lips, then revealed an orchid from the fold of silk over her heart. It was clothed in the same colors of her áo dài. She brushed my tousled hair – I bowed as I felt each strand obediently weave into braids. She nestled the orchid in my hair.

When I lifted my head and eyes up to her, she was gone.

Instead, I saw Chị, her husband, their young children, and many other families approaching.

THE TREEHOUSE

16 Chị held my face in her hands and wept onto my head, "Lan ơi! Em có sao không?"[51] My right hand could feel the scabs and blisters of the 左 character on her left cheek. I pulled my head back to see clearer, but it looked as painful as it felt against my fingers. The labyrinth of lesions bled down her face. We no longer looked so alike.

She was more beautiful now than ever.

I kissed her. All I could do was kiss her. When I touched her neck and shoulders, the chill on her body stung my palms. Her skin felt cold like Khang's illness.

"Chị, you're unwell. You must rest." I slipped away from Khang and swept out another space between the tree's hundreds of legs. I had expected to find spiders and scorpions hidden everywhere, but I saw none.

As Chị, her husband, and their two small children made a home in the banyan's womb, other villagers did the same and filled the tree's rooms. Some people I recognized, many others were new to me.

---

[51] Pronounced roughly "gaw sow kong", meaning *are things well?* or *is there anything wrong?*

"Em ơi, where are Vinh and Khoa? We haven't seen them since our last day in the village." Asked Anh Minh,[52] Chị's husband.

"They went to find food," I explained, "but how did you find me?" I asked, wondering if they saw the orchids, too.

He pointed out the blossom in my hair, "Then it truly was you who shouted to follow the flowers. I knew it was your voice," Anh Minh then glanced back at me, "but how did you know to trust them? How did you know the imperial army couldn't see them? And where are they from?"

"I actually didn't know," I admitted, "I just trusted." I was ready to explain more and ask about Bố Mẹ when Anh Vinh returned. He dropped a stick wrapped in meat, ran to Chị and embraced her and her family. I picked little leaves from the vines as the Beautiful Woman had done and brought them to Chị, "please eat these, they will make you well," I explained, still just trusting.

I spent the rest of the day picking more leaves for the gathering crowd as they built a new village within the banyan's wings. Many of them were falling ill from their infected branding.

Anh Khoa also returned, and hai Anh roasted their catches for everyone to have a little meat.

---

[52] Pronounced as spelled, a proper masculine name.

The smells, sounds, and peace reminded us all of home.

In the evening, the tree hummed with us as we prayed the Rosary. We decided not to light any torches, to keep hidden, but we did have men keep watch from throughout the higher points of the banyan.

It was late when I finally started to fall asleep, tucked in with Chị's children, but nearby in another pocket of the banyan, I could faintly overhear Chị and Anh Minh tell hai Anh about Bố Mẹ, in the quietest of whispers.

I wished it was only a nightmare.

FED TO THE FOREST

17 *Vinh – after you had fled to the forest with the crucifix, Bố was shot trying to save you from the archer. Bố was hit in his shoulder, and Mẹ held him as long as she could before they were separated.*

"That was your imbecilic son who interfered and fled." The mandarin said – he had heard Bố call out for you to run. "Not only did you raise an ingrate, but a coward. Peasants like you are why the Empire falls victim to cockroaches from Europe." The mandarin then spat at Cha.

The army then marched us all to the mandarin's camp. We were grouped and tied to each other by sex, and he marched the women first. After a few hours, we stopped somewhere in the forest.

It was not the camp.

He had said it was for a break, but it was only a break in the dense jungle.

We found ourselves in a round clearing, walled in on all sides by bamboo thicker than rat's hair.[53] Throughout the field,

---

[53] Thickly grown bamboo was often used as a village's defensive walls. Bamboo's fast-growing and extremely tough nature made it very difficult to clear or penetrate (or escape). Việtnamese villages

clumps hung from poles and stumps, and the posts were all higher than any of us could jump. When the wind shifted, we couldn't stand the odor. I puked immediately – many of us did... the smell was so horrible that I wanted to suffocate instead.

I wanted to see why it stank so horribly, so I looked through my tears. I watched soldiers untie Bố Mẹ from their groups and shove them out to the middle of the field, to an empty pole. They were tied together to it, wrists and ankles, tied so they could only kneel and not stand up.

"These parents raised an ingrate and a coward of a son." The mandarin announced to us all, "In order that their son's stupidity is redeemed, they will now provide a valuable lesson for us all to witness, that good might indeed come of their son's evil... as your perverse religion teaches is possible."

The soldiers then took turns emptying themselves on Bố Mẹ. The sound of splashes and pooling filled the silence of the field. I did not want to watch, but I could not stop myself. I hoped Bố Mẹ would remain quiet, so the mandarin and soldiers would not have the victory of hearing them beg or cry.

They did not make a sound.

We even thought they were already dead, since they were so silent.

But then Bố screamed.

I don't remember him ever screaming when I was growing up.

---

used this protective tactic even as late as during the Việtnam War.

I screamed with him.

The soldiers had sliced open Mẹ's womb, and our baby sibling spilled out onto her knees, into the puddles of hot urine. She trembled and struggled to pick up her fallen child, but the ropes cut into her flesh the more she fought.

They clawed out the afterbirth from her and smothered Bố's mouth with it, stuffing up his screams. He vomited it out and they laughed at him.

The soldiers laughed at him.

Then they tied our groups to the remaining poles and stumps. They marched on without us and did not return until the next day, leaving us to watch Bố Mẹ và Bé die slowly overnight, listening to animals eating them in the darkness.[54]

Nobody slept that night. In the morning we could see the only things left were the ropes still holding down some of their skeletons.

---

[54] *Và*, pronounced roughly "vah", meaning *and*.

FORGIVEN MUCH

18 I saw Bố Mẹ in my mind all night, and imagined my lost sibling. Whatever tears I had were already gone by dawn. I watched the sun sneak its way into the forest and begin its day. Finally, I snuck away from Chị's children and went to see Khang. When I found him, his eyes were already wide open, staring into the treetops.

I just looked at him.

"I heard your sister's story last night." He finally said.

I only looked at him.

"Now that I see the Imperial Army from the outside, I cannot understand why we did what we did to so many."

I thought of the demons Cha mentioned in his past teachings: *they are Legion, and they are many.*[55]

"Do you believe your Chúa can forgive even me, for having done such things..."

Pater, dimitte illis: non enim sciunt...

"I don't know why Chúa can, but I believe He does," I said, after waiting for the words. "Since you too can see the orchids, I know He has forgiven. And since you saved Chị, I know you can be trusted."

---

[55] See Mark 5:9.

Khang turned away his face, but not before a teardrop traced down his temple. We sat together silently until I noticed his color had returned to him and his breathing was stronger. I laid my hand on his wounded leg, but he did not flinch.

He turned back to me and sat up, rolled up his tattered pant leg, and brushed away the crusted blood. Only dull scars remained.

I was shocked, but he was even more so.

Chị surprised us, "Have you seen Anh Minh? Our brothers?" She asked with worry. I realized that they had not been seen or heard since last night.

Khang reached for his bow and quiver, but they were nowhere to be found.

MISSING MEN

19 "You must take me!" I shouted at Khang, but he only continued sharpening bamboo poles into arrowheads and shafts. "You must!"

"Ủa, cái gì vậy?"[56] Someone said, coming near to us from elsewhere in the banyan. Neighbors were overhearing us.

"This is very dangerous: your brothers and your husband have gone to challenge the warriors of the Imperial Army. I know their training." Khang looked at Chị and me, "and I do not know if I will even find them alive."

"All the more reason for me to go bury them!" I cried, "at least let me bury my brothers, since I couldn't bury Bố Mẹ!" Chị held me as I yelled.

"I do not even know if I will return alive!" Khang finally said, louder than I had ever heard his voice. He continued preparing a new bow, but I broke away from Chị Vy and ran off to hide my tears from the growing crowd.

---

[56] Pronounced roughly "ooah, gai zee vay", meaning *Huh? What's going on here?*

"Lan ơi, come back! Lan ơi!" I heard Chị call out to me, but her voice soon dissolved when I stopped at one of Anh Khoa's traps. He had taught me to read his trap markings long ago, and they were small sticks twisted together and bent the same number of times as there were sticks. Sometimes the markings would be by chance, but it was always best to check around for a tense vine, cord, or sharp spikes behind leaves.

And there it was: a spread of pointed bamboo tips on either side of a tense vine, to catch anyone who would trip over it.

And there it was: a new orchid trail blooming before me, just like the one we followed the nights earlier. I watched it stretch into the dark forest, curving off, still so similar to the dragon puppets we paraded with in town during Tết.[57]

I raced along the path, kicking up silvery blue petals that reminded me of the Beautiful Woman's áo dài.

---

[57] Pronounced roughly "Det", meaning the traditional Viêtnamese celebration of the Lunar New Year. It remains the culture's greatest and most festive holiday.

THE OTHER PRIEST

20 I slowed as the orchid trail thinned. When there was only one remaining blossom, I knew to start looking for what was being revealed to me. The edge of the jungle was not far, and there was no place to hide beyond the treeline. I searched from safety, listening and smelling, when I heard familiar coughs and smelled familiar fruit.

I tracked the coughs to folded shadows kneeling on durian husks. The mandarin's camp was quiet and still in the distance, and I wondered if they had all gone to comb the forest for us.

Cha Roux was not alone. There was another Cha tied to the same post in the same way, but on the other side. I crawled carefully to them. The odor was worse than Chị had described.

Cha's cassock was steeped in sweat and blood, and puddles had soaked him up to his thighs in waste. He was stooped forward as far as the rope would let him, and his arms were stiff as teak branches. I could see mosquito bites pocked his neck, face, and head everywhere, even inside his gaping mouth. I leaned to his ear and whispered, trying not to startle him, and ants crawled out of it, "Can you hear me, Cha? Please, Cha don't be dead..."

His body still rose and fell with his breaths, and he turned slowly to face me. Cha's eyes were gone, and rusty streaks ran down from their hollow sockets. They looked like emptied mangosteen rinds.[58] He coughed deeply, echoing as a cave, trying to speak.

"Bé... Bé Lan..."

"Cha ơi..."

"How are you... here? Are you visiting... from Purgatory?"

"No Cha, I got away. I'm safe."

"Your parents... too?"

I could not answer.

"I watched... I saw them enter... Paradise."

"Cha... why did Chúa only save me? And not all of us? Not you?" I finally cried. I did not understand. "And now my brothers are missing, looking for revenge."

"Bé Lan... remember... this life... is only for showing where... where you seek to be. Your life... shows what you chose..."

Cha had always said that. He always said so much.

"Cha... let me help you." I cried, tugging on the knots. He shook with each pull, but the slime on the ropes slipped off my grip – their black shine looked like leeches.

---

[58] Mangosteens (*măng cụt*, pronounced roughly "mung goot") are tropical fruits with a deep purple and velvety feeling rind. The segmented flesh inside is bright white, sweet and tart.

"My hour has come…"

I refused to believe him and hurried to one of the burned out barracks. I snatched broken arrowheads and came back to find Cha motionless. I cut him free anyway and rolled his body to the side, out of the puddles. I started to cut free the other priest when he spoke, "Bé Lan, you must stop your brothers, before it is too late."

I noticed his head was scalped and pecked with holes, and his back and sides were shredded into sheets of red and black ribbons – a blend of cassock and flesh. His voice was calm, and his tiếng Việt[59] was better than Cha Roux's, even better than Bố or anyone I knew.

"Cha, let me help you first." I said, reaching for the knots around his hands and feet.

But there were no knots.

I tried to understand what I saw, but when I saw the holes in his palms and soles – I froze.

I stared.

His eyes turned up to mine and saw into me.

"Do whatever My Mother tells you."

---

[59] Pronounced roughly "deeng Viet", meaning *Viêtnamese language*, with *tiếng* meaning sound/speech/voice, and *Việt* referring to the Viêtnamese nation/culture/people/region.

TALITHA

21 I knelt in the puddles, sinking into them with shock, but they became fountains of clear water with lotuses afloat. The rotten post burst into a bouquet of fragrance and blooms, and Cha Roux's cassock filled with white lilies. Even my rags changed into an áo dài not unlike His Mother's.

But He was gone.

I watched flowers pop around me, and plucked one from where Cha's hand would have been. He was also gone – nothing was left but ivory petals.

A swift wind lifted the lily from my fingers. I followed the petals with my eyes until I saw three silhouettes in the jungle nearing the camp, each holding bows and spears.

I crouched behind the bouquet from view, but where I could still see soldiers as they stiffly opened the bamboo cages. Several unbound prisoners crawled in slowly and sat comfortably, shifting carefully behind the bars. The shine of blades caught my eyes before they disappeared under scraps and sleeves.

The guards even left the cage doors poorly tied shut, ready to be forced open with enough effort.

But from far enough away, the prisoners looked desperate for escape and rescue.

Then I noticed the guards were actually loosely bound at their wrists and ankles, but bound nonetheless.

They were not imperial guards.

Those were not Christian prisoners.

In my mind, I heard Anh Khoa whisper the markings of the trap I watched them set for my brothers. I saw Anh Vinh's silhouette in the treeline, nocking and drawing his bow, aiming for the false guards.

I sang out as loud as I could for everyone to hear:

> *Bóng mát í i che đầu, Mẹ...*
> *là như... bóng mát í i che đầu,*
> *Dưới nắng những ban trưa,*
> *trong mưa bao đêm sầu,*
> *Mẹ vẫn che đầu...*

> *Khốn khó dắt con đi,*
> *Gian nguy đưa con về*
> *Mẹ mãi chở che...*

> *Mẹ là như bóng mát,*
> *như làn hương thơm ngát*
> *như dòng suối êm đềm.*
> *Cho suốt cả đời con...*

65

luôn sống vui bình an...
sống vui bình an...[60]

Soldiers circled me as the mandarin approached me. I repeated the song as long as I needed to distract them, and confuse my brothers.

No arrows were loosed from anywhere.

I squinted at the mandarin when he asked, "Bé gái, làm gì đây?"[61] His face bore the scabbing scar of Anh Vinh's arrowhead – it was like a red slash across a bánh bao.[62]

"Picking flowers," I sang happily, offering him one. He took it with a grin, and I stood up, moving my steps so I could see where my brothers were in the distance. I swayed as I hummed on with the song, picking more flowers.

"Cha Mẹ con đâu?" He asked.[63]

You murdered them.

---

[60] This Việtnamese Marian hymn continues with a second verse: *Mẹ là cây xanh thắm, che người đi trong nắng, mau về tới quê nhà. Cây lá tỏa ngàn hương, con sống trong tình thương, sống trong tình thương.* See HolySmack.com for video and lyrics.

[61] Pronounced roughly "Beah gai, lahm zee day?", meaning *Little girl, what are you doing?*

[62] Pronounced roughly "bun bao", meaning a steamed white flour bun stuffed with spiced pork, egg, and sweet savory Chinese sausage.

[63] Pronounced roughly "Jah Meah gon dau?", meaning *Where are your father and mother?*

"I'm alone," I said wistfully, walking away from him and toward the cages. He followed.

"Your dress is so very beautiful, a flower itself. Your family must be of great importance and status. What is your surname?" The mandarin asked. I was unsure how long I could avoid answering.

Give me the words.

"I'm not supposed to tell." I said with a skip, playfully. The mandarin was surprised. I hopped to where they had tried to brand Chị. I tried not to stare at the burnt barracks with glee.

"Perhaps I can guess..." He said. I could tell the mandarin saw something he recognized. The soldiers shrank their circle around us. "Was it not your sister who escaped branding the other night? You both look and sound so very much alike, despite your years apart."

The mandarin waved his hands.

Soldiers seized me and handed a hot brand to him, but I did not try to escape.

"And are you not the girl who cried out to... *follow the orchids*?" The mandarin peered into me, even after I had closed my eyes at him. I hated his eyes on me. "Yet, my army and I never found a single orchid... until now." He brushed his knuckles across my cheek.

"Release her!" Khang shouted from across the courtyard. His arrow was aimed at the mandarin, and several archers aimed instantly at him.

67

BURIED ALIVE

22 "Relax," the mandarin said to his archers, "lower your bows... Đặng Lực Khang, the Prodigal Son, merely returns to beg his father for forgiveness."

I looked at Khang with eyes wide, but he only stared down the mandarin.

"What father leaves his own son for dead?" Khang said through his teeth.

My eyes trembled for him.

"A father shamed by his own son's incompetence!" The mandarin roared, "Caught by silly peasant traps, then becomes a traitor, and even now... the boy further dishonors his father! Either have the courage to shoot, or else show loyalty by eliminating these perverted Christians!"

"Lan! Chạy, em!" Khang shouted, but I was frozen stiff, "Lan ơi!"

The mandarin grabbed my hair and tossed me aside to his soldiers. With sword drawn, he charged his son, but then deflected my brothers' shots with the blade.

"Get Lan! Get her out of here!" Khang shouted at my brothers as he drove the mandarin away. I saw Anh Vinh and Anh Minh shoot their way through, but did not see Anh Khoa anywhere.

An imperial soldier dragged me away, carrying me the way Anh Khoa always carried me. Anh Vinh and Anh Minh shot the soldiers around us as we ran through. When I finally looked closer, he was Anh Khoa all along, "Lan có sao không?" He asked. It really was Anh Khoa, but dressed in a soldier's uniform.

He hid me in the treeline. Anh Vinh and Anh Minh caught up to us, but they were confused, "Why are the soldiers not pursuing us?"

It was quiet all around, and we could hear Khang and the mandarin clearly:

"You were our best archer, one feared and respected by his brother soldiers, and now a Christian sympathizer? Imagine my shame, you selfish child!"

"If you saw what I have seen, Father – the miracles... you too would leave everything behind and follow..."

"*Follow*? Did I not raise you to lead and to conquer?" The mandarin was stunned, "how far you have fallen, for the poisons of this false and perverse religion... for the charms of a pathetic peasant girl!"

"Lan is the greatest of the miracles!"

"I see... I no longer have a son."

"But I have found a true Father."

The mandarin turned away from his son and left. I watched archers throughout the camp bury Khang alive under arrows.

TRAP MARKINGS

23 Khang's body held each arrow out like the spines of a sea urchin. I did not want to turn my gaze, but Anh Khoa took me in his arms.

"We must go, we must go now!" Anh Vinh shouted, arrow nocked alongside Anh Minh's. But we could not go far.

Perimeter sentinels closed in around us. I could tell they were too many for my brothers' emptied quivers. They bound us and held us until the mandarin arrived on horseback. He said nothing for a long time.

"You stole away my only son." He finally spoke. "You Christians, with your myths that appeal to ignorant and base minds... you infected him. I thought that by studying your book and rituals, I could ward off your lies from our people, from my own family..."

The mandarin turned away, "I see now, the only solution is to exterminate you all, lest you spread your perverse, false religion." The mandarin then turned to me – to only me.

"You will take me and my army to the hidden Christians. I know they must not be far. Or else, you will watch your brothers be fed to the forest."

The soldiers tied me onto the saddle of the mandarin's horse. My brothers were locked in a cage and carted along. I looked into the jungle before me, with the mandarin behind me, his body pressed against my back.

I shuddered with disgust.

I searched the distance for an orchid – if one would betray us. *Would one appear, now? Even for him?*

"I see nothing," I said.

The mandarin pushed us forward into the forest anyway, aimless. After some time, the ground became rocky, steep, and unknown. We were all silently moving.

"I said I don't see anything."

The mandarin just continued ahead.

"We will go until you change your mind."

"I can't change my mind, I don't see any flowers!"

"We will go until you see otherwise."

We went over a hill and started down a thick slope.

The sky then started to overwhelm the jungle's shadows. Soon, even the jungle floor ducked away before a cliff. The sky above became also the sky below.

The mandarin just went on, his horse and army obedient and unhesitant.

My brothers groaned through the tight bands across their mouths as the edge neared – step after step. I searched the landscape for orchids – desperately.

71

Just one.

A flower.

Any flower.

But none.

Then the mandarin stopped, just a careless step from tumbling off the edge. We stood higher up than any of the treetops far below.

He uncovered an orchid hidden from within my hair, just a few petals left of it. He tossed it over the cliff and let the wind take it – like a little dove it fluttered off, finally crossing before a trace of rising smoke in the distance.

I knew we all saw the smoke when my brothers started groaning again, yelling through their shut lips.

The mandarin turned and his horse thundered down the side of the cliff. His army charged just behind. Their noise crashed everywhere like a waterfall. It was not long until my brother's cage and its cart bashed into boulders and broke apart.

"Leave them!" The mandarin demanded, only storming forward.

I turned to look for my brothers, but only saw the raging soldiers on horseback stampeding like a mudslide of logs and boulders.

THE ABANDONED BANYAN

24 I had hoped that the smoke was from someone else, from another village or camp. I clenched my teeth and hands, praying my hope was true.

But the forest only grew more and more familiar as we neared.

Anh Khoa's traps sprang around us as we rushed through, snaring horses and spearing soldiers. I did not know if I wanted a trap to catch me or not – whether it was better or not, I could not decide.

But the mandarin decidedly cared nothing for the many traps surprising his army.

Soon, I smelled the smoke. It was from cooking. The plumes grew denser and denser, fogging the forest in a grey shroud. The sun peeked through the canopy, lighting the fog into bright clouds.

Our banyan tree stood surrounded, covered with laundry lines, makeshift hammocks, woven mats and screens, dozens of campfires, and now the mandarin's army.

But no one else was there.

Soldiers dismounted, encircling the giant tree, and from his horse, the mandarin inspected the nooks between its legs. I looked where he looked, and saw what he saw. I searched with my nose and ears, and could smell the fresh food and crackling wood. I could hear the frantic footsteps and panicked breaths.

Dozens, maybe hundreds hidden.

Yet we saw nobody.

The horses paced – spooked – but the soldiers pressed into the tree, climbing it and scaling its steep legs. The tree's many dark gaps gaped wide and vacant, swallowing our stares.

"What sorcery is this?" The mandarin whispered. He gripped my head in his enraged, shaking hands, "giải thích..."[64]

But I was speechless.

"Giải thích!"

I was too shocked to even whimper.

Then I saw her.

We all saw her.

She stood just beyond the tree's biggest branches, and she looked into me. Her lips moved silently, but I heard her voice burst my heart.

The mandarin approached her, raising his finger against her. His army obeyed and advanced. But she just stood there, holding close her infant Son.

---

[64] Pronounced roughly "zai tick", meaning *explain*.

"Who are you?" The mandarin finally demanded.

She turned away and walked.

Her áo dài shimmered in the fading afternoon light, darkened more because of the forest's thickness here. Yet, the silk of her gown glowed warm like a faint ember.

We watched her disappear further and further, effortlessly, without touching a leaf or branch, or stepping around a stone or stick.

The mandarin silently gave chase, like a moth to a flame.

The Weeping Wilderness

25 The mandarin and his army upturned every stick and stone, crashed into every branch and leaf, but they never came any nearer the Beautiful Woman. I saw her little Son peek around her arm at me, and I longed to come closer, but not with the mandarin and his men.

They pursued the Boy and His Mother into the evening, deeper into the jungle than I had ever gone – than I had ever known existed. The dense wilderness had made the horses trudge slowly, almost a crawl. The darkening woods slowed everyone to the speed of wading through water. I remembered the stories of the darkness, and only fixed my eyes on her, ignoring the moving shadows among the trees and caves.

We went where no one went. The forest became covered in clouds of ink that made everything hard to see, everything except her. Some soldiers fell away when they heard sobs echo around us endlessly. Others heard the cries as a stir to further taunt the woman's wailing – obsessively allured. But I never heard her.

"It's all only the wind! All charge forward!" The mandarin commanded wildly.

But there was no wind.

The jungle's packed trees and vines made even breathing difficult.

"Your honor, we cannot see who we pursue."

"We know not where we even are."

"Let us camp and reconsider tactics." Some soldiers said.

"You are cowards in the dark – she is clearly visible in the moonlight!" The mandarin scolded.

But there was no moon.

There was not even a view of sky in the thicket, and I could see they had lost track of time. I could not even guess how long it had been.

"Hear how near she is – hear her screams! We are upon her!"

But the only screams were his soldiers'.

More men fell behind, and only his elite warriors continued with the mandarin's madness. I went along helplessly, listening to their war cries, unable to tell if it was them or the wilderness weeping.

Eventually, only a handful of men remained with the mandarin and me. They were exhausted and stopped for a breath, but their eyes were bloodshot with bloodlust. I looked around and saw the other soldiers in the distance behind us – wandering and moaning like blind men unable to find one another, unable to find their way out.

77

Then orbs of light glowed slowly through the fog. The warriors bolted to them – into hives of fireflies that flew in different directions before leaving us in blackening fog. The men vanished into the shadows without a sound. The forest swallowed them all.

The mandarin dismounted, looked around him – the jungle's wild weeping coiled in on him. He held his ears shut. It was then I saw, between the faint flickers of fireflies, how his robes had been ravaged and his face savaged with a thousand cuts. His ears dangled like torn chicken wattles. He fell to his knees, full of screaming.

The Beautiful Woman stepped out from the shadows with a silken train stretching from her áo dài, swirling behind her far into the forest. Within the mantle of her train were the soft, rested breaths of many that I somehow recognized. I heard Mẹ, Bố, Cha, Khang, my unborn sibling, and so many beautiful voices in the choir. The wilderness calmed in her presence, and the darkness shied away where she went.

With her infant Son close, she approached the mad mandarin, spoke gently, longingly, "Why do you persecute my Son?" Her tender voice seeped into my heart, "Why do you persecute my daughter?" I forgot all my pain.

She turned her face to mine and loosed the bounds around my wrists. Her touch was like a warm bath on my hands. She walked with a peace that I now understood. The horse faithfully followed her steps, carrying me away from the dark.

We left the mandarin alone with his weeping.

APPENDIX
THE EDICT OF EMPEROR MINH MẠNG
(1833)

For many years men from the Occident [the West] have been preaching the religion of Kitô [Christ] and deceiving the public, teaching them that there is a mansion of supreme bliss [Heaven] and a dungeon of dreadful misery [Hell]. They have no respect for the god Phật[65] and no reverence for ancestors. That is great blasphemy.

Moreover, they build houses of worship where they receive a large number of people, without discriminating between the sexes, in order to seduce the women and young girls; they also extract the pupils from the eyes of sick people. Can anything more contrary to reason and custom be imagined? Last year we punished two villages steeped in this depraved doctrine. In so doing we intended to make our will known, so that people would shun this crime and come to their senses.

Now then, this is our decision: although many people have already taken the wrong path through ignorance, it does not take much intelligence to perceive what is proper and what is not; they can still be taught and corrected easily. Initially, they must be given instruction and warnings, and then, if they remain intractable, punishment and pain.

---

[65]Pronounced roughly "Phut", meaning *Buddha*.

Thus we order all followers of this religion, from the mandarin to the least of the people, to abandon it sincerely, if they acknowledge and fear our power. We wish the mandarins to check carefully to see if the Christians in their territory are prepared to obey our orders and to force them, in their presence, to trample the cross underfoot. After this, they are to pardon them for the time being.

As for the houses of worship and the houses of the priests, they must see that these are completely razed and henceforth, if any of our subjects is known to be guilty of these abominable customs, he will be punished with the last degree of severity, so that this depraved religion may be extirpated.

Secret Annexe to the Edict:
Intended for Mandarins and Officials only:

The religion of Jesus deserves all our hatred, but our foolish and stupid people throughout the kingdom embrace it en masse and without examination. We must not allow this abuse to spread. Therefore we have deigned to post a paternal edict, to teach them they must correct themselves. The people who follow this doctrine blindly are nonetheless our people; they cannot be turned away from error in a moment. If the law were followed strictly, it would require countless executions. This measure would cost our people dear, and many who would be willing to mend their ways would be caught up in the proscription of the guilty.

Moreover, this matter should be handled with discretion, following the [Confucian] maxim, which states: 'If you want to destroy a bad habit, do so with order and patience,' and continues:

'If you wish to root out an evil breed, take the hatchet and cut the root.'

We order all tổng đốc and all others who govern: [66]

1. Carefully to attend to the instruction of their inferiors, mandarins, soldiers, or populace, so that they may mend their ways and abandon this religion.

2. To obtain accurate information about the churches and homes of missionaries, and to destroy them without delay.

3. To arrest the missionaries, taking care, in doing so, to use guile rather than violence; if the missionaries are French, they should be sent promptly to the capital, under the pretext of being employed by us to translate letters. If they are indigenous, you are to detain them in the headquarters of the province, so that they may not be in communication with the people and thus maintain them in error. Take care lest your inferiors profit from this opportunity by arresting Christians indiscriminately and imprudently, which would cause trouble everywhere. For this, you would be held guilty.

We forbid this edict to be published, for fear that its publication might cause trouble. [67]

---

[66] *Tổng đốc*, pronounced roughly "dong doc", meaning *governor*.
[67] "Minh Mang on ridding Vietnam of Catholicism (1833)." *Alpha History,* https://alphahistory.com/vietnamwar/minh-mang-catholicism-1833. Accessed June 17, 2025. Corrections, explanations, and modifications mine.

Reflection Questions

The following questions guide deeper exploration of the Legend,
or aid group discussions:

Chapter 3: Which group of villagers is correct: those who
want to restore the chapel as a shrine of idols, those
who want to disguise it, or those who want to keep it
as is? Why?

Chapter 4: Why is Cha tolerant of the mandarin stepping on
his face? Why does he tell Bà that he is nothing?

Chapter 6:

1. Although the Church permits Catholics to receive
Communion only twice in one day, why do you think
Lan receives all the hosts at once?

2. Why do you think Lan describes the "full moons" as
becoming "new moons"?

3. Who is the woman Lan refers to when she receives
Communion? How is she relevant?

4. Why do you think Lan only receives Communion
with her mouth, and does not touch any Hosts with
her hands?[68]

Chapter 10: Why are Lan's brothers suspicious of the young
soldier's prayer? Is it ever just to do such a thing?

---

[68] This scene was inspired by the true story of an anonymous
young girl who did the same as Lan, but during anti-Catholic
persecution in China. The story was made famous by Archbishop
Fulton J. Sheen when he explained why he always devoted an
hour daily to adore Jesus Christ in the Holy Eucharist. For the
story, see his autobiography *Treasure in Clay*, pp. 126-127.

Chapter 12: Why do you think so many cultures regarded the "left" of anything to be flawed or wrong? Why is this belief unjust?

Chapter 13: When did the Virgin Mary historically use other miraculous flowers to help and guide? Why flowers?

Chapter 15: Why are Infant Jesus' hands and feet wounded here, although His Passion happened when He was an adult?

Chapter 16: Why does Lan think Chị Vy is more beautiful than ever with the scars?

Chapter 17: People of all nations have committed great evils to others during war (and even not during war); why do you think this happens? How can it be prevented?

Chapter 18: Why do you think Khang and the soldiers thought their violent acts were justified? What leads us to do such things to others?

Chapter 20: Who is the other priest? Who does he echo in his last words to Lan? What do his last words reveal?

Chapter 21: How does this chapter's title "Talitha" relate to the chapter? What's the reference?

Chapter 22:

1. How does the parable of the Prodigal Son relate to the mandarin, and how does he misuse the story reference?

2. How is Lan the greatest miracle for Khang's life?

3. What makes a man into a true father? How does that relate to our Heavenly Father?

Chapter 25:

1. When the mandarin is lead to his demise, what Biblical events do it allude to?

2. Who is the Virgin Mary echoing in her last words to the mandarin? How does it relate to the allusion?

3. How could the mandarin have been redeemed?

4. Why do you think the mandarin weeps in the end?

5. What do you notice about the last page of this chapter? How does it relate to the ending scene?

Ending Thoughts:

1. How does the book's opening quote from John 2:5 relate to the entire Legend?

2. How does the opening sentence of the novel go full-circle? How does it relate to what the Virgin Mary does with Lan? with the mandarin? with Vietnamese Christians?

3. When does Lan start using the young soldier's name in her narration? What do you think causes the change?

4. After reading the Edict in the appendix, what are some misunderstandings the Emperor may have had about Christianity? What are misunderstandings that nonbelievers may have today about the Church?

ABOUT THE AUTHOR

Evan Phạm, when not reading, writing, or teaching in the classroom,[69] spends life as an outdoorsman. He hunts, bikes, hikes, camps, and kayaks in God's country. He also designs holy cards, writes a blog, and runs a small online shop with his own custom Catholic apparel, blankets, puzzles, decor, and prayer cards at HolySmack.com.

His favorite foods are the Việtnamese dish from Chapter 1 (mom's, of course), tourte au poulet from *Douceur de France*, *WOW* strawberries, wild blueberries from northern Michigan, katsudon from *Take Sushi*, black tonkatsu ramen from *Shiromaru*, kimchi cream udon from *Izakaya MEW*, Detroit-style pizza, grapefruit *San Pellegrino*, milk tea from *Molly Tea*, and a ceylon-assam milk tea blend from *Sangaria* (almost impossible to find).

Look for Evan's next book on another Marian apparition.

P.S. As of this book's publication, Evan's car has over 423,000 miles on it. Onward to half-a-million!

---

[69] Mr. Pham's past courses include Church History, Apologetics, Mariology, and Prayer & Discernment. He currently teaches literature, theology, and philosophy at a classical Catholic academy. His students also call him by many names: *Phamily, Phammy Pack, Phammunition, Phampire, Phamtom of the Opera, Phamazon, Phamsterdam, Phamtastic, Phamster, Phampoo, Phamnesia...* despite *Phạm* pronounced roughly "Phahm".

AVE MARÍA
GRÁTIA PLENA;
DÓMINUS TECUM:
BENEDÍCTA TU IN MULIÉRIBUS,
ET BENEDÍCTUS FRUCTUS VENTRIS TUI
IESUS.
SANCTA MARÍA, MATER DEI,
ORA PRO NOBIS PECCATÓRIBUS,
NUNC ET IN HORA MORTIS NOSTRÆ.
AMEN.

KÍNH MỪNG MARIA
ĐẦY ƠN PHÚC
ĐỨC CHÚA TRỜI Ở CÙNG BÀ,
BÀ CÓ PHÚC LẠ HƠN MỌI NGƯỜI NỮ
VÀ GIÊSU CON LÒNG BÀ GỒM PHÚC LẠ.
THÁNH MARIA, ĐỨC MẸ CHÚA TRỜI,
CẦU CHO CHÚNG CON LÀ KẺ CÓ TỘI,
KHI NÀY VÀ TRONG GIỜ LÂM TỬ.
AMEN.